T0084395

Rescuers

of Skydivers

Search Among

the Clouds

Rescuers
of Skydivers
Search Among
the Clouds

A Novel

Patrick Lawler

FC2

TUSCALOOSA

Copyright © 2012 by Patrick Lawler
The University of Alabama Press
Tuscaloosa, Alabama 35487-0380
All rights reserved
Manufactured in the United States of America

FC2 is an imprint of the University of Alabama Press

Book Design: Illinois State University's English Department's Publications Unit; Director: Tara Reeser; Assistant Director: Steve Halle; Production Assistant: Emily Moody
Cover Design: Lou Robinson
Typeface: Garamond

♾

The paper on which this book is printed meets the minimum requirements of American National Standard for Information Sciences—Permanence of Paper for Printed Library Materials, ANSI Z39.48–1984

Library of Congress Cataloging-in-Publication Data
Lawler, Patrick.
Rescuers of skydivers search among the clouds / Patrick Lawler. — 1st ed.
    p. cm.
ISBN 978-1-57366-168-3 (pbk. : alk. paper) — ISBN 978-1-57366-832-3 (electronic)
I. Title.
PS3562.A867R47 2012
813'.54—dc23
                                2012013877

For my teachers, mentors, muses, jesters. Cross-pollinators, metaphysical spelunkers, wiccan mycologists, and web weavers; spiritual hoboes, shamanic cryptographers, and tantric storytellers. Thank you for your work, your advice, your support, your inspiration, your laughter—and mostly your love.

"A child of nine or ten sits at the edge of the crowd, alone, playing on a wooden flute."

—Ursula K. Le Guin
"The Ones Who Walk Away from Omelas"

Rescuers

of Skydivers

Search Among

the Clouds

MY MOTHER
WALKED DOWN
JOY BOULEVARD.
MY FATHER WAS
A BEEKEEPER.

That year the mayor decided to name the streets after presidents who had been assassinated. He was never satisfied. According to him a town's character was written across it in the names of its roads. Once the streets were named after berries, so we walked down Choke Cherry Lane or Elderberry Road or Raspberry Way. These names gave us places to live our lives. Girls could be lusted after on Strawberry Street. Boys could smoke cigarettes, watching clouds of hair from the corners of dark red/blue intersections. The mailman would lug his bloated bag down Boysenberry. Places for estrangements and entanglements. Places to meet people or leave people. The mayor made a conscious effort to select the edible berries though some poisoned ones slipped in—which led him to go with the assassinated president idea.

When I was born they named the streets after emotions: my mother walked down Joy Boulevard. My father was a beekeeper.

Almost robotic among the bees with his smoke pot and his bee clothes, almost feminine with his netted face. I spent my childhood with bee stings. My mother was a hagiologist studying saints. My sisters would spend afternoons digging for relics in the backyard. The bees were ambassadors from an ordered and enchanted world. They were scholars obsessed with an ideal, always returning to the same roundish, yellow perfection of their lives. Flying alchemists. I know they were important doing their honey dances. I loved and hated them at the same time.

It was impossible to tell whether we lived in the sky or lived in the earth.

All the while, I practiced magic tricks. It was the only time I wasn't afraid though I wasn't very good at making things disappear. But I'd call the family together and I'd try hard to make things invisible. It became apparent that I needed practice. My oldest sister played church music. Every day after school this God-sad music would drown the house.

Every Thursday we practiced fire drills. That was when the phrase "Whatever" was first used with its current connotation. I was in love with this girl in my class. I lived for her, the sky of her eyes, her movement, her voice. I told her all this, and she said "Whatever."

I forgot to tell you we lived in the ground. A glass rain fell around the House. One day I wrote a poem and my mother sprinkled holy water over everything. This was years before my brother became invisible. I didn't know that he had been secretly rehearsing.

It was impossible to tell whether we lived in the story or lived in the words.

My father asked us to practice fire drills. Every Thursday we knotted sheets together. We would crawl on all fours beneath the smoke from his smoke pot. We memorized the exits. We imagined the linoleum would go gooey with the heat. We practiced breaking glass. One day I would make a list of all the people I didn't save.

My mother always felt something really good would happen. Years later my father became a bee sipping from an aluminum flower. Mostly we ate honey. My sisters came into the house with these tiny saint bones in their hands. I called the family together for the Magic show. I didn't have a veil big enough.

It was impossible to tell whether we lived in the filled or lived in the empty.

That was the year they named the streets after the elements: I walked down Fire Lane. One day I would make a list of all the people I wouldn't save. My father was getting pissed because I wouldn't write the book. I just said I didn't have anything to write about. Would you come to live on my side of the moon? I said to the Whatever girl. I couldn't keep her from vanishing. During one of the fire drills my father made a fire out of my poem. "This will make things more realistic," he said to the family. Then he turned to me. "Now you'll have something to write about." Nothing is as happy as it sounds. That was the year my mother felt certain she was going to win something. She would be cleaning the house for the day they would arrive with the prize. My older sister's music ate holes in the house. You see, nothing is as sad as it sounds.

MY SISTER SOLVES
THE RIDDLE OF
THE MINIATURE HOUSE.

That was the year my father bought parts of a used miniature golf course. Once he began setting it up in the back yard,
he noticed that it was essentially broken. The windmill had no
blades. Paths were worn in the green felt. A clown's chipped
mouth flared. He plopped his red toolbox next to a pile of wood.

Part of the problem was we couldn't distinguish between a
dream and an egg. That was the year we kept losing things. My
mother kept losing the prayer we would say to the patron saint
of lost things. "Look," my father said. "We can make a lot of
money. People have to play miniature golf somewhere. Why not
here?"

"Every daughter needs to study how fire moves through a
house," my mother said, moving her finger over the blueprints.

My father arranged the ramps and cups and miniature train
tracks and tunnels and mazes on the green felt carpets. That year
I was afraid of being lost. The birds carried bright pieces in their

beaks. After my father said there wasn't enough food, I began eating like a cricket.

That was the year we couldn't find one of my sisters. The mayor wanted to name the streets in my father's tiny town. That was the year we hired a person to find us. My father patched the roofs of the miniature village. He collected the golf balls in a bucket, and painted the fake lighthouse so its light would always appear to be on. He hammered paddles on the windmill, and the balls rolled under the porticoes and around the gazeboes. "I'm not sure what you want me to do," said the man we had hired to find us.

I wanted to cry in front of my grandmother's bookcase. The world was waiting for me.

The weather spun around the woodpile of my father's town.

My grandmother watched food wake up on her plate.

"Don't listen to her," said our father.

The words in my grandmother's bookcase pretended to be what they said they were.

In my father's village, he painted a door over the word "door."

After painting the clown's mouth, my father's hands were bloodred. Once a fire started in one of the miniature buildings. "You'll never guess where I found her," said my father looking away from my sister.

"You don't know anything about golf," my mother said.

My father spent all of his time with buckets of paint and bags of nails.

My mother said, "The holes are *supposed* to be there."

"Don't walk in the backyard because you might step on a nail. Then you get lockjaw," my father said. "And you don't want to get that, or you'll go crazy and die."

We walked carefully among the boards that gleamed with the silver tips of bent nails as my father called us out to admire his brightened world. When my father handed her a bucket of balls, my youngest sister said it looked like a pail of eggs. After the birds left us behind, my mother made up some words to say to the patron saint of lost things. No one said that my father's world still looked broken.

All I know is I didn't die, and one of the houses had a hole in it where a fire had been. Next to my grandmother's bookcase I imagined a word rolling slowly toward the thing it longed to describe. My mother said the trick was to determine which holes needed to be patched and which ones needed to be there.

THE ORNITHOLOGIST STANDS WITH HER HANDS CUPPED TOGETHER— PALMS UP—WAITING TO CATCH WHAT SHE IS CERTAIN IS FALLING TOWARD HER FROM THE SKY.

We discovered our neighbors didn't close their shades when having sex. One body turned into the round ball of the other body. Each brain a piece of flint; each body a piece of flint.

Because my father was a Student Driving Instructor, he always came home with bruises on parts of his body that had been slapped against the dashboard. He used hand signals when talking to me about sex.

At night, our neighbors gnawed on each other.

We were floating bits of time. I didn't know why anyone would wear a welding dress.

ASK THE HOUSE.

That was the year one of my uncles said he was into kinky sex, "After sex I get a kink in my neck, in my back, in my leg."

During the day our neighbors yelled at each other.

The TV said: You are so wrong and couldn't be any wronger.

The Meanwhile Girl lived in a world that was ample and ebulliently fleshy. Afterwards, empty, exhausted, our neighbors became stumps.

ASK THE WINDOWS.

There would be no noise behind the glass. We would have to imagine sound, and I thought it would have to be humming.

My brother left a note on the kitchen table. It said: I suspect suicide will play a role in my recovery.

In town the Dream Palace Theater played the same movie over and over. The screen sulked behind the jittery light.

ASK THE FIRE.
ASK THE WICK.

One of my uncles had a tattoo of a naked woman. Eventually after becoming real, she was a naked woman who was once a tattoo. One night she came to my bedroom—on her arm was a tattoo of a tiny man.

My father showed us where the seat belt had dug into his neck. We lived next to the conservancy, and everyday people walked by with violas strapped to their backs. I decided that was how I would one day make love—with a musical instrument strapped to my back.

"I doubt that," said the Meanwhile Girl.

In winter we watched the windows overflowing. It was like watching the movie in the Dream Palace Theater, except there was no sound—or the little sound there was seemed muffled and foreign. Behind the glass and behind the snow the two naked neighbors touched each other—animals trying to grow wings— radiant and disgusting and mute and resonant. It was as if the flakes of snow floated upward. Oh. We could not look away.

BODIES MOVE
INTO EACH OTHER
LIKE BIRDS
INTO A WINDOW.

We told our parents that we wished we had been adopted, so then we wouldn't feel so bad about our lack of feelings toward them. Our father said, "It will pass—this lack of feeling thing. I know. I've felt the lack myself. And though it takes awhile, eventually it diminishes."

That was the year the school play was *Death of a Salesman*, and we looked for hoses in the basement.

If we had been adopted, my oldest sister said that maybe we weren't real siblings. My brother said parents should come with evidence.

That year a letter arrived in the mail.

That was the year my mother suspected my father had an affair with a toll booth operator. My father always had pocketfuls of quarters. My youngest sister grew next to a mirror. "I wonder what would be a good name for a mother," she said.

In my grandmother's bookcase was *The Book of Knots*.

"Why do you have to be so negative?" my father said. My mother made a list of the ways the world could come to an end. She placed it on the refrigerator with a magnetic sunflower growing out of the supervolcano. At night we imagined there was a sky above us.

My brother left a note on the kitchen table. It read: "I want to find my logical parents."

"We should always be prepared," said my mother.

"Exactly," said my father jiggling his pockets.

Every time I poured a glass of milk I stared at the words "pandemic." I always felt I lived in a town called Disappearance. My mother said no matter where you are you need to find the spots where God slips through. Every time I opened up the refrigerator door, I witnessed climate change. The book said: A knot is just a string trying to find its way home.

My father said he had to travel the thruway again, and my mother asked him where he was going. I stared at the refrigerator and felt the cosmic ray from an exploding star, sensed my telomeres eroding, heard a black hole gulping.

"How can I be a traveling salesman if I don't travel?" said my father. My mother pulled the hose off the clothes washer, so that the water splashed on the floor.

"Such beauty," my mother said. "The way we are so completely uncertain while the earth, arriving at a purposeful clarity, sorts things out to the point where, given our presence, it embraces the purest inevitable conclusion."

Our "father" and "mother" called us together, and said they had something to tell us.

THE PERSON
WE HIRED
TO FIND
LOST THINGS
BECOMES LOST.

I attempted to talk backwards—to have words go back into me—over the teeth and plump tongue, and finally down the trap in the throat. My father worked as a Fool the Guesser when the carnival came to town. That was the year somebody was stealing books from the library.

I was afraid of electricity—the way it snapped inside things unexpectedly. The spark could come out of nowhere. I decided to take books from the library and place them in my grandmother's bookcase, and then exchange that book for one of hers. The TV said: Nothing is real.

My father looked at my younger sister quizzically. "Dad, I'm eight," my younger sister said. In school we studied phobias. That was the year we couldn't find the right words—fear or worry or alarm or panic or apprehension or dread or fright.

Just before the carnival was scheduled to arrive in town, there was a greenish spill from the chemical plant.

The TV said: There is nothing to be concerned about.

The cellar crackled—every outlet, every appliance. I jumped.

With a razorblade I took off the inside pocket that contained the library return card. Then I glued it to my grandmother's book, and took it to the library. That year I ate like a pencil.

For school we had to make a list of things we were afraid of. My list included:

ELECTRICITY
FACTS
BREATHING TUBES
GETTING CAUGHT

I tried to move words around until they resided in their original mouths. I sat with my head in a book. "Thank god it is only his head," said one of my aunts. "Wouldn't a lightning rod make sense," I asked.

I wanted to learn to play a musical instrument. I wanted to learn how to fall.

When they set up the carnival tents in the greenish pool, the clouds in the sky appeared crushed. Believing in books, I had forgotten I was a real person. At night the narrator started talking. At the carnival, the phrenologist read the bumps on our brains. In the cabinets of curiosity carefully constructed worlds came to life like butterflies on the ends of pins. I tried to throw balls through the mouth of the greenish clown. "Step right up."

Apprehension.

"Wouldn't a lightning rod make sense?" I asked.

My father said to my brother, "Don't be a smart ass. It's not just the Fool. You have to add the Guesser. Fool the Guesser."

When the storm eventually came, the thunder sounded like panic cracking in two. A whole terrible and beautiful world gushed through me. Lightning ripped open the sky as the green clown sucked the world back into its laugh.

The TV said: Look at the pretty. The TV said: There are no consequences.

The TV said: Worry.

Later my mother stood in front of my father. He looked at her intently. "OK. Not pounds but what about kilograms? You got to admit," my father said, "I'm getting better."

My mother grew alarmingly heavy.

I could hear my grandmother when I'd bring her new books to read by her hospital bed. She made a dreadful sound as if she were vacuuming up all the words. That was the year, when if you touched anyone the static electricity startled your skin and you jerked back. When I gulped everything seemed to go backwards. The electricity ran through the TV and ate a hole in the living room.

**MOST OF US WILL DIE
FROM COMPLICATIONS
FROM OUR TREATMENTS.**

I lived in a cellar. A house grew out of my belly.

THAT WAS THE YEAR
MY PARENTS BEGAN SPEAKING
IN A STRANGE LANGUAGE.

That was the year I developed a variety of theories about time. I wanted to think like a train. I wanted to move like a hill.

My father said my brother was a doorstop. My older sister bumped into an inexplicable brightness.

ASK THE HOUSE.

ASK THE TOWN.

That's the year one of my uncles overflowed behind the windows.

"He deserved it," said my father.

I tried to hold onto a piece of who I was, as the Therefore Girl flickered past the lockers. I wanted the original. The neglected. The myriad. The world quite frankly needed the world. That was the year our neighbors gave their children away. Garage sales everywhere were filled with doll clothes and broken appliances and stone clocks with garnet gears.

One of my grandmother's books explained how to become

a window. I practiced when I walked next to the shops of the town in the simmering noon sun.

In school I learned the first flying machine was an apparatus made of birds. I learned narratives illuminate the neural connectors of the brain.

If you looked deeply into the cellar you could see a crater where the heart of the world had been taken.

We awakened in a dirt house.

We awakened with rumors of the sky.

We awakened in tomorrow holding onto a very old root.

ASK THE WINDOW.

I felt the weight of time as it moved through the clock. There was the glow of rumination. The TV cranked out its beam of light. A world was building itself around us. The sadness of architecture spread over the sidewalk. There were holes in the town that no one could ever fill.

"We never saw it coming," said my mother, and for the first time I saw a tremble in her hand as she opened the letter that had come in the mail.

That was the year the school orchestra couldn't afford musical instruments, so we made music from boxes and sticks.

Nature was dying in our backyard. We kept digging holes bigger than our own bodies. When I walked I felt as if the town could see through me.

ASK THE TREE.

ASK THE STONE CLOCK.

The TV said: We are telling the truth.

In school I learned there would be transition stories—stories between the old stories and the new stories. I stood in front of my grandmother's bookcase. I had forgotten how to read.

At one of the garage sales my older sister purchased a mirror that reflected the town and the hill and the hole where we lived. All of it was caught in the glint of the sun.

We didn't see any birds, so we suspected time had gone away.

THE BIRDS
GIVE UP
THEIR WIGS.

Learning this technique from my grandfather, we wore bird costumes when we interacted with the birds.

We named pets after members of the family, so when we called my brother he would come and so would the dog. In the same spirit, my mother searched for two-for-one sales. And when we called my youngest sister, the fish with the same name floated through the plastic castles.

My brother said he was going to become an existentialist, and I stared at the silences around him. "Now what can I do?" he asked. "I've become the wall I built to protect myself." The words were attached to nothing.

In school the teacher asked us to draw a self portrait. "It doesn't even look like a person," said my teacher. "More like an animal playing a flute."

"I don't get it," said my father. That was the year he worked in a cough drop factory, and walked around with lozenges stuffed in his pocket.

One of my aunts hated bees, so she hired an exterminator. He came with a pump canister with a thick dark red tube like an artery attached to a spray nozzle.

My mother announced that she wanted to draw birds down from the sky.

The neighbors were always drunk, and it would scare them when they saw my sister set her dolls' hair on fire. The neighbors would swing wildly from gleefulness to despair and then back to something resembling a stumbling ecstasy. Always they seemed disconnected.

That was the year the window salesman came to town.

The Dream Palace Theater taught us every moment is the same moment only with different resonances. The window salesman taught us to look.

Insecticide dripped off my aunt's house—down the shutters, down the eaves. Big poisonous tears. The bees came out of their drowned house—stunned, transfigured in the glaze of chemicals.

The exterminator was a conjurer of an alternate world of luminosity and need. "You don't realize how bad things can be," he said. "Something has to be done."

The hives were drenched paper tumors.

My mother said what we loved we had to pull out of the sky. Oh, how I wanted to be normal. Little did I realize normal was the problem.

That was the year the pets kept dying—first the goldfish, then the cat, then the dog who slept under a truck.

So we began to have funerals for the pets that were named after us. And my father brought my brother and me two pigs. He said they were our pets and we could name them.

The goldfish slid beneath us inside the pipes.

My brother looked at my aunt's house and explained the sensation, "It is as if an airplane has run out of gas." When fall came, my father helped to direct the pigs into the truck. It didn't seem right to eat the things you named.

When my mother looked at my drawing, she said, "It is as if I have dreamed it. And I'm not certain I mean that in a good way."

Our grandfather sat in his wheelchair with birds all over his shoulders and lap and head. When my grandfather started coughing, the birds shook from him like pieces of coal. My father handed him a cough drop and smoothed the feathers on his arm.

My aunt dreamt she carried a bag of broken bees. They sounded like my father's pockets.

Nothing flew around my aunt's house.

THE HEALER
EVENTUALLY
BECOMES AFRAID
OF HER HANDS.

"They're really not mine," she insisted—the blackened nails, the cracked skin, the knot of each knuckle. She glared at them as if they could not possibly belong to her. A sore garden, a withered mood. Still, her hands made her sick. More like roots. She wished there was a way to get back to the original illness. When she approached, her mother moved away.

THE WAY GLASS
VIBRATES SLIGHTLY
AFTER BEING TOUCHED
BY LIGHT.

"Words hurt," said my Grandmother.

"Words hate us," said my brother.

Standing in front of my Grandmother's bookcase, I felt the vibrations and hunger. Each book nudged its way into the next book—one book being eaten by another.

"Words collect in the corner of the mouth," said my older sister.

That was the year when there was an accident in the library, and we were thankful we lived next to a mirror factory.

These are some of the books I saw in my grandmother's bookcase:

> *Book of Stuttering*
> *Book of Disease*
> *Book of Light*
> *Book of Fears*

Book of the Sequestered
Book of Erotic Tortures Designed from Butterflies
Book of Skin-maps
Eclectic Book of Sleeping
Book of Breath
Book of the Ethereal
Book of Licking
Heavy Book
Book of Everything that is Not in the Other Books

When I looked at the *Book of Falling Things*, a part of me was falling. When I looked at the *Book of Flying Things*, I knew there was a part of me that had already flown.

That year in school we studied obsolete medical practices, like leech therapy, wound movement, pupil massages.

One of my aunts had hair like a tumor. It grew higher and higher on top of her head.

When we walked past the mirror factory we walked past ourselves.

For some reason I was drawn to trepanation. The teacher said it was because I lived in a cellar.

A man who was in the library accident was buried under classics. When they tried to rescue him they started drilling down through the books and lowering mirrors to see if there was any breathing.

My brother said he would never drill a hole inside anything.

"What if it could save somebody?" my mother asked.

In the library they tried to yank the man out from under the words, but it was futile. Eventually they had to give up. When they recovered the body they held a mirror up to his mouth. It was a tiny piece of sky.

I discovered eight words appeared in every book in my grandmother's bookcase: nudged, vibration, wound, massage, trepanation, food, pear, spirit.

I kept reading: I sucked on the spirit as if it were a bitten pear.

My grandmother was worried. "God is getting incredibly old." She cautioned me, "Believe everything you don't read."

In the library, in the aftermath of the accident, I sat in the blaze of the However Girl. My aunt with the tumor-like hair looked into the book-hole that had been created from the incident. She nearly toppled over.

My grandmother said, "Life is unbelievable."

That was the year the Mirror Factory looked like a dark lake.

That was the year something terrible happened to my Grandmother, and my mother said that in order to save her they would have to open up her head and insert a light.

I'm not sure exactly when it happened, but instead of eating, I read the *Book of Food*.

WORDS YANKED
OUT OF SILENCE.
I WAKE UP INSIDE
BOOKS.

I was the one the family hired to tell jokes. We hired my
sister to play classical music. It was as if Beethoven were being
stabbed. That was the year my father dreamt my mother died,
and she kept asking him questions. "Was it a terminal disease?
An accident?" "Was it lingering or sudden?" My father kept
turning over the coins.

I was certain that if everything forgot me, I would no longer exist.

My oldest sister had the name of a man tattooed on her
arm. "But you don't even know anyone named Ludwig," said my
mother. "I'll find him," said my sister.

We lived next to a bird sanctuary—so we knew what it
sounded like to be starving.

We hired a stranger to be the Perfect Child. Looking at each
of the children and then pointing to the Perfect Child, our parents said, "Why can't you be more like him?"

We placed a scarecrow in front of the cellar to keep away the house.

We put our father's suit on a stick.

That was the year my father collected coins. He would pour them on the kitchen table and announce that they would be worth something some day. My mother tried to hide her disappointment. "You see this one?" said my father. "This is the one." It seemed more silvery than the rest.

That was the year we hired my brother to walk away.

Birds grew into the sky, music filling their bellies, Mozart stumbling into the cellar.

That year a letter arrived in the mail.

My father said, "What the hell happened to my coin?" I didn't want to tell him that somehow it had found its way into the pocket of the Perfect Child. I thought it would be best if my father discovered that himself.

In the bird sanctuary there was the sound of starving birds.

Everything looked for food.

My mother said she didn't think she could take it any longer. She went to a fortune teller who in her flowery dress looked like she came from the branches.

"You cannot build a house of happiness on someone else's house of sorrow," said the woman who looked like a bird. "Oh, and by the way tell your husband I know who stole the coin."

With more than a little guilt, I watched my father send away the Perfect Child. He turned to me, "Now you'll have something to tell a joke about."

A new family moved next to the bird sanctuary. "What's your name?" my sister asked the boy.

WHERE THERE'S
SMOKE THERE ARE
FIREFLIES.

That was the year we practiced for emergencies. Fire alarms were always going off. Emergency crews gathered around the fake purple chemical spill next to the train tracks. "Cool," said my brother. "Kool Aid," said the mayor.

After the church was struck by lightning, the priest claimed the stained glass saints began to dance.

I couldn't tell whether my mother said the future was attacking us or attracting us.

That was the year my youngest sister turned her doll house into a funeral home. That was the year snipers set up outside the lunchroom, and we were told they had blanks. Still, the red Jello shivered like targets as we slid them along on our trays.

My father sold storm windows, and there was always broken glass on the front lawn.

That year my brother set fire to the toilet paper in the school bathrooms.

"Government regulations require compliance," crackled over the school intercom.

A Handbook was handed out to everyone in the town: Five Ways to Make an Emergency Fun:

1. *Turn tragedy into a positive experience.*
2. *Know the exact location and time of day when the most people will be injured. Do not go to that location during that particular time of day.*
3. *Determine your readiness quotient.*
4. *Remember tampering with or disabling monitoring equipment is a violation.*
5. *Never walk barefoot in the front yard or your feet will be bloody.*

In school that was the year we studied synchronicity. Our neighbor worked at the animal shelter—putting them to sleep, cradling them with a syringe. That was the year we wrote Thank You notes.

After my uncle was struck by lightning, his penis wouldn't stop growing.

That was the year the rescue rope unraveled.

In the mock Emergency Bomb Scare Drill, ambulance drivers, police, doctors, nurses, cleanup teams, and firemen arrived in biosafety moonsuits.

In the fire drill, we learned to drop and roll. With the fire extinguisher, they sprayed the backs of the students as they emerged from the toilets. We learned to survive weather. In the Nuclear Drill, people practiced running. No matter what, we practiced holding our breaths. During the Terrorist Drill, we learned how to identify people who were different. During the Emergency Operation Planning, my father carried a stopwatch. I slept in a positive pressure suit.

I had a big empty sack inside me.

A hole was discovered at the center of my grandmother's books.

A storm shattered all around us.

My brother said he was searching for his birth mother—I thought he said bird mother.

After the library was struck by lightning, the characters in the books came to life.

I always felt like something on the verge of having a name. "Ishmael?" I asked when I saw a slumped man emerge from the library.

I wanted to be a victim just once. I thought I looked good in fake blood.

My father, fearful of every bump and pothole and swerve, drove a glass truck.

EVERY TIME
THE DICTIONARY
SWALLOWED

I lost another word.

I CAN'T PUT IT
INTO WORLDS.

That was the year I listened to my parents pushing around a boulder in their bedroom. That was the year of the Air Show. Planes bumbled in the sky until they became small. Eventually they vanished, and then reappeared from behind thick clouds— behind metallic flowers. Planes hummed into sky-holes.

That was the year I kept hearing my mother say no. My youngest sister hid the keys, and my brother wore a pair of gold sneakers.

Propellers with their big stuttering blades churned up the air.

When the bookcase broke, I could hear my grandmother's books shatter into words.

My father was a children's performer who made extinct animal balloons. After he blew and stretched and twisted, he'd pull out a very large needle and announce, "We must get used to the sound of bursting."

That was the year we lived next to a polluted lake with the Map Factory on its shores.

My mother asked my grandparents what color they wanted their deathbed to be. My grandmother said she figured out how to stop time.

We discovered a stranger in our backyard, the parachute having fallen around him like some gigantic silk flower. He looked exhausted.

Though the children's parents appreciated my father's dedication to reality, they rarely invited him back.

The planes thumped against the clouds.

That was the year I ate tiny almost invisible wings.

The Therefore Girl wore a bruise-blue dress. I wanted to ask her a question, but the words kept drifting away.

I watched my grandfather swallow a mouthful of time.

We lived next to the Map Factory. The machine that made the dye for the rivers broke. The machine that made the dye for the lakes had a leak, and the color ran down to the water.

The planes formed configurations as if they were recreating a mythic alphabet over the polluted lake. Eventually, the planes landed, opening their cockpits, and the pilots fell out.

"Gold," said my grandmother. "A beautiful gold."

The sky folded itself over the horizon. When the map factory closed down, we lost parts of the world.

I could hear my mother's No come from the darkest part of the cellar.

Every night I grew a pair of wings; every morning they rotted away.

THE MACHINERY
WAS PUT IN PLACE
TO REPAIR
A BROKEN SKY.

That was the year my father's twin died. At the funeral my father started wearing a disguise, so the family could tell them apart, and the one who looked like my father was dead, and the one who did not was alive.

That was the year the bees started to disappear.

My father walked around as if he knew he were disappearing.

The biplanes in the sky kept traveling until they became small musical notes. The gasping motors. The rattle of the propellers. The TV said: This is the real world.

The TV said: This is the fake world.

The doctor wrote my father a prescription. As my mother arranged the herbs on a shelf, she fell in love with the names: St. John's Wort. Valerian Root. Damiana. Clove Tea.

In school I studied flight.

That was the year my father started wearing disguises in order to distinguish himself from the dead. He began to look more strange. When he sat down for dinner, he pushed in his putty nose and began to speak with a German accent.

"What are you doing," asked my mother.

I was too afraid to laugh.

Notes from a pad were scattered around the house with words written in a strange script: Wellbutrin. Effexor. Prozac. Zoloft.

I opened *The Book of Grieving and Harvesting* in my grandmother's bookcase. She asked me to read it aloud.

The TV said: This is clarity. This is otherness. This is what a lie looks like.

The birds flowed like consciousness.

The stream on the side of the "house" meandered like a doctor's signature. That was the year everything existed within quotation marks—especially my "father."

For the midterm I memorized the flight patterns of migrating birds. It didn't take long before we forgot what my father looked like.

Once a bird flew into a window. Eventually it grew out of its reflection. There were strange side effects:

The woods silently grew in back of the house.

Inside the tree, someone had inserted the forest.

In the woods at night I could hear my pulse.

The TV said: I am the border between the real and the real.

The TV said: I am the border between the real and the fake.

When she looked into the darkness behind the house and the woods sang itself to sleep, my mother asked, "What shall become of us?"

A man with dark glasses and a fedora pulled down over his ears, with a thick broom-like mustache and a bulbous nose, stood in the shadows. "Dad?" I said, and my "father" shriveled up behind his hat.

I BEGAN
LOSING PIECES
OF MY STORY.

"It will be different this time," said my mother. And the smell of baked bread filled the kitchen.

That was the year we dreamed in lists. We spent most of our time pretending we were happy. When our neighbor was an arsonist, we kept a fire extinguisher in every room.

When our neighbor was an aerialist, we stretched a wire between TV antennas.

ASK THE HOLES.

My youngest sister buried parts of dolls in the backyard.

A retired astronaut lived next door. He used a walker to move from various pieces of furniture.

In school we studied how to change the world, but I didn't do that well on the exam. That was the year I set the fires but put them out immediately.

Our neighbor was an accordion player—his whole body acted like a bellows. Our neighbor's grandfather was a stick man who walked hunched over.

That was the year there was a fire in the belfry of the town hall. With the smoke pouring out, it looked like a steam ship.

Our neighbor was an inventor. In her yard there were a number of things that felt awkward because they knew they shouldn't exist.

That was the year I learned to count backwards. I witnessed all that was leaving. I wasn't sure whether our neighbor was an opportunist or an ophthalmologist or an optimist. Then I saw the gigantic eye chart. My mother said no one could miss seeing a single letter.

That was the year our neighbor was a prison guard who frequently lost the handcuff keys.

One of my aunts had hair that looked like a tumor—and my father unrolled a road map. "Now this looks like a good place to be," said my father.

ASK THE EYE.

ASK THE THING THAT IS SEEN.

ASK THE THING THAT FLOATS BEHIND THE EYE.

My sister buried a tibia, a fingernail, a tiny tip of a plastic tongue. That was the year a transvestite lived next to us, and he took my brother under his wig.

There was a fire in the firehouse. No one was alarmed.

There was a fire in the choir loft. No one had a prayer.

I wasn't sure whether our neighbor was a spiritualist or a survivalist—he meditated in his bunker among cans of sweet corn and peas. A gas mask hung on the wall next to the dream catcher.

My mother rearranged the letters on the eye chart so it said:

HELP

There was a fire on the map, and the place where my father wanted to be burned down.

That was the year we learned our neighbor was a shrink. My father blamed him for attracting crazy people to the neighborhood. He was larger than I suspected.

My father looked angry when he saw the smoke rising around my hands.

We discovered a pilot's leather helmet and broken bits of balsam wood in the backyard. After our neighbor's son died, I thought he said, "I just want to feel whole grain." Water came out of our neighbor's eye. "It will be different this time," said my mother.

THE HOUSE
THAT LIVED IN
THE GROUND.

"Thank god, we live in a cellar," said my mother. "We avoid all those things that would crash into a house."

My youngest sister danced on the roof of the cellar.

"We don't have to be entangled in trees and sky. Birds don't have to crash into us," said my mother.

When my sister stood on top of the cellar, she became the house.

THE TIME-FLIES FLEW AROUND
MY GRANDFATHER'S FACE.
"TIME-FLIES," SAID MY DEAD
GRANDFATHER, AND HE MADE
A HUM SOUND WITH HIS CLOSED
MOUTH.

Time was a thing.
Time was a being.
We couldn't decide.

THERE WAS MORE
SPACE FOR SPACE
THAN THERE WAS
FOR WORDS.

My mother wanted to dance, so she went to dance lessons and never told my father.

That was the year we bought a microscope, and we watched the world as if it were rinsed in a washed out purple, as if it were tinted in pink. My brother said, "That's not the world." And we knew we shouldn't listen, but I guess we already had.

That was the year my sister placed a recorder in the empty hive.

"Where are you going?" asked my father.

My brother said he kept watching me think about what I wasn't going to say. "It's disturbing," he said.

We lived next to the pet shop. That year we studied cartographers of imaginary places, and our cages ached.

My father arranged my sisters (chronologically, alphabetically, acoustically) and ordered them to sing.

While the world happened around me, I buried my head in my grandmother's books.

That was the year my mother's dance shoes sparkled. That was the year they mined the air for a particular light—and it was perfect.

My grandmother's bookcase bulged like a tomb. *The Book of Invisibility. The Book of Ancient Burial Practices. The Book of the Body in a Box.*

As my sisters stumble-danced, my mother did the tango around the weeds in the yard; she did a boxy fox-trot around the kitchen table; she waltzed and waltzed—and was excruciatingly happy.

That was the year the transvestite came to town, and the dance shoes ate the choreographer's brain. The dance shoes ate the rain. My brother left a letter on the kitchen table: I will not be available.

My father said, "I'm not sure how you learn to dance with a broken leg," and my sisters sang like diamonds.

My mother said, "If I have to, I will dance in my own tears."

My sisters began humming like bees to commemorate the sound we no longer heard.

KNOW
THEIR KNOT.

The house was hiding.
The house was hiding in the cellar.
The house was broken.

"Too many fires for the irons," said my grandfather.
That was the year we underestimated the weather.
That was the year I was accused of stealing.

The volunteer firemen came to put out the fire in the dollhouse.

God had a flashlight. What a joke.
We trained the birds to tie our shoelaces.
We pruned the windows.

Our neighbor wore a monocle.
The clerk from the hospital consulted the *Death Book*.
Our neighbor repaired bicycles. The lawn was filled with chains and gears and handlebars.

One of my aunts wore jewelry like sparkling teeth.

I was accused of stealing.
The parachute looked like a floating rooftop.

"Look," I said. "I have nothing in my pockets."

If you just let things go, then everything will be…
In the background we discovered a broken propeller among the rubble.
I could hear the buzz in our backyard.
"I don't think you can have sex without a body."
"Not stories but simultaneities."

If you will only admit it. I don't need to see.
The interrogator whittled.

"What do streams want?" asked my mother.
The indentations. The sanctity of the empty pocket.

Broken bicycles rattled through the shaky town.
Of course, what you have stolen doesn't have to be seen to be used as evidence against you.

WE DETERMINED THAT THE MUSIC PLAYING IN OUR HOUSE WOULD BE EXACTLY THE SAME MUSIC PLAYING IN OUR CELLAR.

"What are you trying to say?" said my mother. The sky was charcoal. One of my uncles worked in a false teeth factory. It was as if the town had dropped out of the sky. Pieces of it were all over the place.

My father was a master of disguises. A biplane. A parachute. The buzz of the missing bees. The thump of satellite parts tumbling back toward the earth. According to my oldest sister an airplane crashed into a window in her dream. Tears drilled their way through my father's eyes.

My brother said he wanted to discover the hidden self inside things.

A letter arrived in the mail.

My father worked in pesticide application—a sweet sickening smell lingered around him. One of my uncles said my father's tears were poison, and I watched my father cry all over the lawn. He planted tiny *KEEP OUT OF AREA* signs all around the yard.

My uncle worked in a false teeth factory. He said the incisors were the hard part. "Molars are easy. Like gravestones."

An airplane creased the glass of my sister's dream.

The Since Girl talked to me after class. Gravity had already memorized her body, and I ran out of things to say. I could feel a hook inside my heart.

As always, rain pushed its way back down through the sky.

When my uncle walked his pockets chattered.

"Keep your mouths shut," my father said to my uncle.

My father fell asleep with plastic yellow rectangles scattered around him. KEEP OUT fell all over my father's body.

MY EYES
TAKE TURNS
CLOSING.

Because my father was a kleptomaniac, my mother always gave me money to leave in stores. "Just put it on the counter and walk away." "But Mom, suppose someone sees me?" She didn't answer.

"It's not right," said my brother. My mother didn't answer.

That was the year we established a relationship with things, and that was the year we studied sadness in school.

"Your father acts just slightly ahead of his time," said my mother. We lived in a town of extraordinary kindnesses, and my grandmother read the *Book of Meadows*.

That was the year I ate erasers. My mother would laugh nervously every time the crop duster flew by, and we ducked. I tried to be a TV show, so I could meet my parents in a later episode.

My father accepted the generosity of objects that were compelled to enter his pocket.

He was a lab technician and would bring home vials of mysterious liquids. That was the year I was afraid of rodents though I would feel guilty every time I'd hear the traps snap.

When my father came home his pockets were full of trinkets. My grandmother explained the enigma behind the activity in her flower garden. The bee would always take something and leave something behind. A benevolent burglary. A sense of mystery and wonder.

That was the year we studied the centuries of sadness. In our house we could never use the word "steal." It was forbidden. We could never use other words. That was the year I ate all the words that had been swallowed by the eraser. Mysterious liquids were arranged on the shelves behind the mirrored door of the cabinet.

"Your father is sick," said someone at school, so I beat him up. I wasn't really defending my father as much as I was defending my right to be the only one in my age group to say my father was crazy. The birds in their own way burglarized the sky.

My grandmother read the *Book of Madness*. In school we studied eighteenth-century sadness, indigenous sadness, Chinese sadness. The sadness in plants. The sadness in starlight. The sadness related to bees.

In the Drug Store I was accused of stealing a Black Magic Marker. I said, "No, I didn't. Check my pockets." "Check my jacket." " Prove that I am innocent." I desperately emptied my pockets, yanking them inside out. The bell went tingting when my father walked out the door.

THE WORLD
WAS A CHARACTER
IN THE STORY
THAT I WROTE.

That was the year I listened to my parents having sex. That was the year we discovered the individuals of the town had rearranged themselves into different combinations of families. "You are not my mother," said my sister to the new woman who sat next to her at the kitchen table.

That was the year I worked in the cemetery, mowing lawns, clipping around headstones. One gravestone said *STONE*. One said *GRAVES*. One said *HEY*.

One of my uncles fell down a flight of stairs. When he hit his head, all he could see was a fantastic light.

I walked around the town and I heard the humph sounds from inside the different houses. The town sounded like a musical instrument in a fire. The sky was the bottom of a dented bucket. And then it rained.

One of my sisters grew next to a mirror; one of my sisters shattered mirrors with a hammer. That was the year we lived next to a telescope factory. When I entered my uncle's hospital room, I was nearly knocked over by the glare of light. My father sold camouflage, knots, and needles. Drunkenness followed my father home. Anger followed my father home. My father sold plastic, aluminum, and Teflon. My father sold bunkers and bomb shelters.

Fear and broken bottles followed my father home.

ASK THE WORLD.
ASK THE ANGEL.
ASK THE STONE.

A fantastic light shone in my uncle's sad eye. The stones in the cemetery seemed to grow backwards. The house would lower itself into the earth, and then in the morning it would rise back into the sky as if it were on a pulley.

If we don't change our stories, we will die. The TV said: Don't listen.

Sadness followed my father home. That was the year I saw a woman lying on a grave—crying.

My father sold the commemorative prayer cards they distribute at wakes. An angel from one of the cards followed my father home.

That was the year I kept hearing my mother say no.

EVENTS AND OBJECTS
SEEMED TO BE MEANINGFUL
BUT NOT WITH THE MEANING
I HAD ASSIGNED THEM.

My mother went to the doctor in order to read the magazines. She started "doing" her hair in the styles she'd find in them. After some complaints from a variety of people, my mother asked the doctor to get more recent issues. "You're looking well," said the doctor, sticking his head around the door to call in another patient. "Especially your hair."

After my grandfather died, my grandmother became a window.

The cellar taught me to fly into the earth. My youngest sister said, "I'm waiting for the cellar to grow into a house."

We couldn't figure out what language our neighbors were speaking. They would yell at us from the other side of the fence. "It takes a village to bury a grandfather," said my mother. Words fell through my grandmother's books.

My father did experiments with Time. "Jesus," my father said. "Where did it go?" I found a door inside one of my grandmother's books. That was the year I forgot which god I was praying to. My grandmother handed me a rosary of bees.

My grandmother's roommate in assisted living stole her things. Eventually all my grandmother's possessions flowed away—her cards, her shoes, and her clock drifted to the other side of the room.

I read one of my grandmother's books—*Book of the Sky*. That was the year there was road work ahead—and my brother distributed anti-war pamphlets.

That year we studied the pre-Socratics.

Various objects (street lamps, signs, etc.) floated in the sea that was the town. Eventually my grandmother's roommate began choking. There were piles of things that didn't belong to her. I could hear the rosary of bees.

We thought the neighbors were offering condolences—but they could also have been responding to my mother's hairdo.

"I'm cleaning clocks," said my father, and he seemed angry.

My grandmother sat with an empty suitcase next to her chair. "I'm going home," she kept saying. When I looked at my grandmother, I could see right through her.

"I'D" HIDE IN
THE MIDDLE
OF HIDING.

We lived next to the pharmaceutical company that was developing a pill that would cure the symptoms that were the result of all the other pills it produced.

The Priest tied helium balloons to the church. That was the year one of my aunts made clothing out of food—and animals followed her around the town. That was the year of laughter.

(laughter)

That was the year when I was hidden.

That was the year I was in moral torment—guilty that any success on my part would undermine the fallenness of those I loved, frightened that any achievement would challenge the lives of those I feared. I was cautiously angry that all of this was true. I felt as if I were being searched for—but I wasn't certain by whom and whether anyone really wanted to find me.

(laughter)

That was the year we read the *Book of the Clown*. My aunt's flesh grew into a house while my uncle carried a red tool box. A sadness hid inside the laughter; laughter hid inside the book. The priest's balloons were in the shape of crosses.

We held our breaths. My mother warned, "If you breathe too hard, you will disrupt the flight patterns of birds."

My uncle said, "It is impossible to build an entirely new house from the scraps of the old." The priest's balloons kept thumping into birds.

In one of my grandmother's books it said: "In the metaphysical comedy, the clown alters our consciousness." My aunt lived her life as if there was a pill that could save her.

That year we studied the secret life of secrets. A room hid inside the house. A bird hid inside the church.

(sadness hid inside the laughter)

The Nevertheless Girl said, "Why can't you be your brother?" And I said my brother has disappeared. And the Nevertheless Girl said, "Exactly."

I wrote as if I were filling a hole. I wrote as if I were building a house—a new house inside another house inside a different hole. I lived my life as if I would never be found.

I HAVE NO WORDS FOR THIS.

In school we studied chloraplasts—where light is turned into energy. My youngest sister took dance lessons, her ballerina shoes sat pinkly in the corner. My older sister pretended she died. "I just want to know how people will react."

My father sold rocks.

My father sold maps.

That was the year we lost my brother. My father said, "It is your fault. You never wanted him to be your brother." That was the year I changed my name.

When I was asked what I wanted to be, I said I wanted to be a drawbridge. I was afraid of forgiveness—the power it had over the one forgiven. That was the year when the roofs of the town collapsed. That was the year we studied light.

My father sold rubber bands.

My father sold plans for the impossible work that needed to be done.

My father sold wedding equipment—all white and drippy.

"Why are we doing fire drills? We live in a cellar," my older sister asked.

"We are preparing to escape the fire of the house that once burned above us," said my mother.

"Just because there is no smoke, doesn't mean there is no fire," said my father.

I prepared myself to be the family eulogist. My youngest sister's tap shoes clicked their way through the kitchen.

"No matter what you call yourself, you are not your brother," my father said. My sister showed me the hole in the wall where the fire lived.

My teacher asked, "Why a drawn bridge?"

My father sold Amway.
My father sold aluminum toys.
My father sold name tags.

I got tired of explaining it all.

My mother sold blueprints. My father sold helium. My mother sold light.

My grandfather had Alzheimers, so my mother put labels around the house. "Balloon." "Refrigerator." "Pot." Eventually everything vanished into the ink of its name. The words became more powerful than the things they swallowed. My brother's name stared at us from the kitchen chair where he once sat.

THE WORLD
OF SAD OBJECTS
STARTS SINGING.

We lived next to the Kaleidoscope Factory, and after the explosion, bits of colored glass fell over the yard for months.

My father was a taxidermist and had glass eyes all over the house. They were always looking.

One of my aunts wore a hive for a hat.

That was the year the trees studied dendrology. The fish studied ichthyology. The rocks studied their own hearts.

At the Spelling Bee I had to spell the word "honey," but I didn't know there was an E.

That was the year I started writing my father's obituary.

The TV said: Watch it.

Things unexpectedly began to turn into other things.

A story became a window.

That was the year we studied hagiology.

It all started when…

    a fish turned into a piece of wood

oranges turned into a small town

hats into hiccups

handwriting into geese

garens into yawns

lightbulbs into bouquets

napkins into sparrows.

I couldn't believe it. The sky caved in under the weight of all the color.

One of my aunts made clothing out of cobwebs.

In my grandmother's *Book of Thought* things began to rattle.

The hook became the line; the line became the sinker.

One of my aunts wore a living hat.

I looked out the window, and my mother asked, "What color is the weather?"

One of my aunts made clothing out of petals.

The book became the line; the line became the singer.

I grew hungry every time I saw my aunt. "I'm so hungry I could eat a road," said my brother.

My mother said, "We must become new kinds of beings." My aunt sprayed herself with pesticide.

It all started when…

a saint became a window

thought became breath

When I spoke it was as if I had a mouthful of glass.

Roads became ideas we couldn't get out of our heads.

My sister's heart turned into a fish.

All around there were deer eyes, owl eyes, bear eyes. I could barely look.

Honey dripped down my aunt's face.

The skydivers wore the sky like skin. When they hit the earth, they shattered into a thousand bits of color.

**THE FIREMAN
CARRIED THE ASHES
OF ALL HIS FIRES
IN HIS POCKET.**

"Here is one I remember," said the fireman, and a crooked-ness quizzically visited his face.

**FOR THE PEOPLE
WHO FELL FROM
THE BURNING PLANE.**

Who provided the rain clouds?

I STARTED SPEAKING IN CODE—IF I SAID EVERYTHING WAS OK THEN IT WAS NOT.

I saw my sister naked and I was amazed. "Are you aware of this?" I asked my brother. I looked at my mother and felt all the energy it took for her to pretend that she was happy.

The flesh of everything was the same flesh—the flesh of the flower, the flesh of an insect, the flesh of the house.

I watched a dart of a bird in the backyard enter the flesh of the sky. The sunset looked like meat. That was the year my mother told us to pretend we lived in a hotel. She put little triangles at the end of the toilet paper. "It's not that hard," said my exasperated mother.

That was the year the hospital lost the body of a fetus.

ASK THE BROKEN.
ASK THE POOR.

We lived next to a florist shop and there were dead flowers piled up everywhere. We laid them at the feet of Our Lady of The Place. I wasn't sure if it was a good thing or a bad thing, but the house became indistinguishable from the sky.

There were certain places in the town we were not allowed to go. "Look at this," my father said. "Evidence."

We lived next to the shadow factory. The TV said: What did you expect?

A SECRET CELLAR EXISTED BENEATH THE CELLAR

My father ran his finger in the honey, as I stepped on the dirt skin of the planet. One of my sisters said, "I will go to sleep among the mushrooms." ASK THE AIR WHEN IT IS TWO INCHES FROM YOUR MOUTH. My grandmother opened a door made of words. The mushrooms grew in the dark like fleshy doorknobs. "Are you aware of this?" I asked my sister. A word thumped against my eardrum. A road thumped against my father's feet. That was the year we fell to pieces. One of my aunts was allergic to bee stings. My father was a sifter. He'd search through material looking for clues. My sister tried on a costume the day my brother brought home a real girl. In my grandmother's books, the vowels prepared themselves to swallow the words. The flesh of everything was the same flesh—the flesh of my sister, the flesh of a word, the flesh of the clues. When we left, the cellar opened itself like a flower. When we entered, the cellar locked itself up like a bud.

THAT WAS
THE YEAR I
FINALLY DIED
IN MY STORY.

That was the year I stepped on a nail

That was the year I hitch-hiked through foreign countries

That was the year I kissed a nursing student in the elevator with
a corpse

That was the year I stuttered

That was the year I couldn't be found

That was the year we cut diamonds with our tears

That was the year the fireflies chiseled up the dark

That was the year of the bone trees

That was the year periscopes appeared in the clouds

That was the year someone else's tongue grew in my mouth

My mother said we needed to prepare ourselves to survive the unthinkable. "How can we do that if we can't think about it?" my sister said.

That was the year I ate like a scarecrow

That was the year I ate like a stone

That was the year I ate like a stick

That was the year my father was on the crew of a hot air balloon

That was the year we read the librarian like a book

That was the year something beautiful came out of the sky

That was the year a child grew out of the snow

That was the year the cellar sank further into the ground

That was the year we lived next to a psychiatric hospital

That was the year the weather reports arrived behind the weather

That was the year the family became parts of speech

That was the year when we lusted

That was the year we learned all life has intrinsic value

That was the year I lived inside a book

That was the year my father did experiments

That was the year I learned to laugh

That was the year I learned not to laugh

That was the year I was trying to survive

That was the year we lived forever

That was the year of the flame

That was the year my father drew a map

"You are here," my father said and pointed to the sky.

IF YOU ENTER THROUGH THIS DOOR YOU MUST GIVE UP THE DARKNESS IN YOUR WHITE HEAD.

That was the year I discovered the inadequacies of language. I thought the sign said:

BEWARE DANCER

That was the year I learned to be afraid of language. I learned my thoughts needed to stay an appropriate size in order to stay inside my head. My mother said the neons were missing letters. One sign said: PEN. But they didn't have one. One sign said: IT. But I had to leave. We lived next to the firehouse, and there were always sirens and smoke and birds.

The neighbor's child was autistic and looked at the sky with frightened eyes. Making a flapping shadow with his hands, my father said my mother was an ornithologist. "For the birds, at least, the sky flies away."

My brother learned to take both roads simultaneously.

My father said, "What are you—stupid?" My mother said, "We'll get your eyes checked."

During the disaster birds fell out of the sky.
I wasn't certain what I was on the lookout for.
That was the year we began writing the obituary.
Language was a conveyance.
That was the year we started diagramming sentences.

That was the year the town decided to put up a monument. A forest without any trees grew next to the town. That was the year the unthinkable sat next to the thinkable. Miracles surrounded us in their ordinariness. Birds were addicted to clouds.

That was the year I ate smoke.
I asked the Thus Girl if we could take turns carrying things.
The room withered in the center of the house.
The sky was excessive.

In one of the buildings, we heard they were experimenting with the heads of animals. The couch fattened in the TV light. Objects were eating us, but we didn't notice. Our shoes made us feel guilty.

The following gifts were not given by my father: a tiara, a toy jeep, a thinking map, a book as a nutrient, an empty briefcase. My mother said the sky is a lake that crashed into a mirror; my father said the earth is a lake that is choking.

"The only reason to jump out of a plane is if the plane is crashing," said my uncle.

"The plane *is* crashing," said my mother. The sky was full of falling.

I saw a wild person stomping in leotards, his arms came flying out of his sleeves.

I wasn't certain if there might have been a letter missing: The sign in front of the church read GOD LESS.

At night the neighbor's child saw heavy bodies drop out of the sky.

My father made a shadow with his clasped hands. My mother called it the hand-bird.

ONE DAY THEY WILL LOOK BACK AT US AND SAY, "WHAT ON EARTH WERE THEY THINKING?"

That was the year we sought to live in a place of hope. (Here was one of the major problems: I couldn't tell the difference. I was a little confused. It came down to sex, death, and food. I knew some were acceptable at various times, and some weren't at all acceptable at other times. Basically, I was in a quandary when I approached the dinner table.)

"You can't get anywhere if you don't have a plan," my father said. He carried a box of black footprints.

That was the year we lived next to a nuclear reactor. The women were told not to have any children. The doctors looked at me. "We told you," they said to my mother. My grandfather's name was entered in the *Death Book*.

A window was the flesh of the wind.

My grandmother had a cancer clock, a cancer stick, a cancer spoon.

We lived next to a pawn shop. We knew what everybody in

the town discarded.

The streets were coronaries. That was the year our school had twenty-three bomb scares. My oldest sister said she took a Psychology course in order to diagnose the family. My father said he was going to start his own band and accordion music squeezed its way out of the cellar. It sounded like pets were being squashed.

The TV said: We are telling you the truth.

In school we studied butterflies and disease. That was the year I learned to eat words. The town said: If we had only known. Between the caterpillar and the pupal stage, the alarm rang. When I returned to the classroom, I thought I heard a ticking.

If I thought about stealing, whatever I thought of wound up in my pocket.

"This is the sky we fall from," said the owner of the pawn shop as he pointed to the jewels behind the dusty glass case. "What's that in your pocket?" he asked me.

The wind lived in windows. My grandmother stirred the bowl with her cancer spoon.

Between the ailment and the cure, the alarm rang.

That was the year there was a chemical spill when a truck tipped over in the center of the town.

My father studied to be a dance instructor. He laid down black footprints all over the yard. That was the year my mother told me I was going places, and my father pointed to the footprints that seemed to move in a box.

We all had our versions of the story.

"We cannot stop entering this town."

"We cannot stop entering this house."

"We cannot stop entering this family."

The town did not expect us. The chemical did not expect the town.

When I thought about sex, the alarm rang. When I thought about food, the alarm rang. When I thought about death, the alarm rang. I listened to the sound of my teacher's clock.

"I said I was hungry," I said when I attended the funeral of my grandfather.

In front of the school, I stood in the snow waiting for the sniffing dogs to tell us it was OK to go back in the building where a butterfly was waiting to emerge from the pages of a science book.

The only way to move forward was in extraordinarily slow, elaborate circles. Dance footsteps grew into the road.

AT SCHOOL I WRITE A STORY CALLED "GENITALIA."

"Mom, nothing's going to happen," said my older sister.

My mother left "Safety Tips" around the house—on the refrigerator, on the bathroom mirror.

> If a robber asks for your wallet, do not hand it to him. Instead, toss it away from you.

One of my uncles had three balls or at least that's what he told everybody. My aunt said he wasn't very good at math. I never had any evidence one way or another.

That year the boys in school tried to look up the skirt of the However Girl.

The uncle who was supposed to have three balls gave nick names to people. He said, "C'mon, I've got an extra nickname."

After our father left, my mother kept putting up warnings around the house.

> If you ever get thrown in the trunk of a car, kick out the back tail lights and stick your arm out the hole and start waving.

After my father left, I heard one of my aunts say to my mother, "That's just the way men are. If he's not thinking about yours, then he's thinking about somebody else's."

That was the year the household went through considerable amounts of Kleenex.

We studied Latin in school. "Let them scoff and make fun," said the Latin teacher. "We'll be the doctors and the lawyers. We'll know the roots of things."

My Latin teacher asked me what I was trying to look up in the dictionary.

> Do not open the door if you hear a crying baby. A man has recorded the sounds of a crying baby and is using it to lure women out of their homes late at night.

"I don't see why you are doing this," my older sister said to my mother.

My uncle always said to my aunt, "You've got food on your face." And he'd point to a spot on her cheek, and she'd brush off something that wasn't there.

The Latin teacher asked, "Why do you keep dropping your pencil?"

My aunt always said to my uncle, "You've got something on your nose." And with his fingers he'd swipe away at something no one else could see.

My aunt kept buying lottery tickets so there were dark crumbly piles around her kitchen table.

My uncle said, "I'll tell you how to treat a woman."

"What about our aunt?" my brother and I asked. "She's a wife," he said.

"I think it has something to do with flowers," said the Latin teacher.

Late at night we heard a baby crying—but no one dared to move.

THE FIRE EATER
BURPED SMOKE.

That was the year my brother hid the *Playboys* in the closet underneath the baseball cards. The second baseman for the Chicago Cubs was particularly impressed. November was a little scared.

That was the year I ate my shadow.

That was the year I ate the TV.

My father blindfolded my sister and sharpened the knives. He said, "But I need the practice."

The sirens were quiet while the library burned. I read the *Book of Trembling*. Knives ate the air around my sister's shoulders.

The left fielder for the Detroit Tigers was bemused. January looked cold.

That was the year I learned how to eat fire. "Tilt your head and don't breathe in," said my father.

My mother asked me, "Why does your brother have this renewed passion for baseball?"

One of my dead aunts memorized all the books in my grandmother's bookcase. That was the year we tried to fly the stone kites. That was the year the fish named the water. The water named the shore. The clouds named the sky. We couldn't tell where we were going.

There was a dying animal in the backyard. "Don't look," my mother said.

In school we studied sorcery and concupiscence. That was the year my sister sang. That was the year the sky was made of rocks.

Living in the cellar was like living in an egg—except there was no way to get out.

All the winged structures weighed down the sky. Oh, combustible August.

That was the year the TV ate us. Oh, sweet September. Oh, the plushness of July.

"Aren't you supposed to wear the blindfold?" my brother asked my father, and he twirled him toward a shaking target.

That was the year the fat fruit growing from the trees in our backyard longed to be eaten. The dying animal named my mother's hands. Whatever was about to be eaten named the mouth.

We lived next to the Statue Factory, and, when the trucks came to pick the statues up, all their blue eyes stared out at us from the crates.

That was the year I encountered the multiplicity of existence.

That was the year I didn't know how long I'd been sleeping.

November with long silky gloves and a burgundy blindfold stepped out from behind the lush target.

MY SHOES
FELL ASLEEP.

We lived next to a hospital, and when it was windy wheel-chairs rolled into our backyard. That was the year there was an accident on one of the roads in town between two trucks, and millions of bees escaped.

That was the year a hole opened up in our back yard, and we gathered around it in fear and awe and started to tremble.

I was in pieces. In school we studied luminosity.

They used smoke to calm down the million bees.

THAT WAS THE YEAR X-RAYS ATE OUR SKELETONS.

It was nearly impossible to remember how to breathe.

ASK THE WORDS
ASK THE STONE
ASK THE LIGHT AS IT EATS OUR BONES

My sister screamed, " Doesn't anyone in this family tell the truth?"

We had entered a perilous world. I had to learn a new language in order to understand myself.

We lived next to a hospital, and when it was windy x-rays blew all over our yard. Gradually my feet would arrive just behind my shoes. Our house grew into the dirt. The birds grew into the clouds. We shared a communal sense of loneliness. One of my uncles looked at the fire in the town hall and said, "Searing is believing."

My sister showed me the hole in her bedroom where the bees came in.
I didn't want to be the one to break it.
Bees kept entering the holes in the vowels of my words.

Because the town burned down, the bees slumbered.
The cellar was a choking bird.
The cellar was a shoe that didn't fit.

My older sister said, "If you stare into the hole long enough, the hole will stare out of you."
We watched the smoke eat the sky, and we grew sleepy.

IF I PULL THE ROPE HARD ENOUGH, THE WHOLE SKY COMES TUMBLING DOWN.

We lived next to an ophthalmologist, and he placed a placard on his front lawn. At first, we thought it was to support the election of the mayor, but then we saw that it was an EYE CHART.

That was the year someone was stealing parts of our house. My father said, "If we are ever to finish the house, we will need to scrimp. Tell me this. Can we afford to feed the older children?" My mother sat silent.

One of my sisters stopped growing. And in spite of the rationing of food, one grew so large my father built her another bedroom.

Trying to catch the thief, my father, dressed as a burglar, sat in the dark.

My mother brought the house to the edge of the river in order to scrub it.

That was the year I pretended to have amnesia.

"I don't think so," said my father.

That was the year something happened that needed to be forgotten.

My sister brought home pictures from the magazines in the doctor's office—taped them to her bedroom wall. "See, I'm normal, and because I'm normal I just want to be someone else."

My brother carried his darkness around with him. "T J Eckleburg," he said. The sky sagged. The words in my grandmother's bookcase were attached to nothing.

We provided blood samples. Urine samples. They made us defecate in a bucket.

The cellar smelled like mildew. Rust. Ashes. Cleaning chemicals.

My mother tried to beat the cellar on a rock.

The best answer I could come up with when I sat in the ophthalmologist's chair in front of the goggles with lenses that clicked into place was, "I don't remember."

My father faced the stranger as he stumble-slid into our house through the window. Both wearing ski masks, they stared silently and with a sense of recognition at each other's darkly circled eyes.

Every night the ophthalmologist changed the lawn chart until the script was tinier and tinier, until everyone in town bought a new pair of glasses.

I GREW MY
PARENTS IN
THE DARK
OF THE CELLAR.

ONE OF MY AUNTS SAID, "I'VE RUN OUT OF PILLS TO TAKE."

When my mother came home, she said she might have hit something with the car. "How could you?" asked my father. "It was dark and slippery." "I mean, how could you not find out? What was it?" "I don't know," said my mother.

In school we studied ventriloquism. And that was when the police showed up. Or at least it sounded like they showed up.

That was the year I ate like an ant.

"Where is it now?" asked my brother. That's when my father told us he was building an airplane in the backyard.

At the family reunion, my uncle drank wine made from bees. Every night I lost my body, and every morning I got my body back. Our neighbors named their horse after my sister, and my uncle drank wine made from holy water and wrung out from religious vestments that had sat out in the rain.

My father was a phlebotomist and walked around with a hypodermic needle. My mother said it was like a thunk and then a muffled scream.

My father brought home a big eraser and said, "Lets see what you've written." That was when the firemen showed up. My grandmother picked her death-flower, and my uncle drank a wine made from birds' wings.

My father planted a garden, and it eventually grew bigger than the cellar, so no one could see where we lived. My mother started crying and never seemed to stop. "Come out to the garden," said my father.

My mother said it sounded like an airplane crashing into the front fender.

The horse with my sister's name said: I am afraid of your father. I wanted to protect the cellar from the garden, the hypodermic needle from the wine.

In the fall when we ate the squash, it tasted like my mother's tears.

The TV said nothing was happening. That was when the ambulance showed up.

It was dark and slippery, and I threw my voice onto the road.

MY FATHER'S
TWO HEADS.

My father lifted off his welding mask and placed it on the kitchen table. It remained there like a dark mood.

MY BROTHER
ASKED US
TO CALL HIM
SISYPHUS.

Being a foley artist, my father had a sound for everything. To make the sounds of cracking bones, he broke stalks of celery. That was the year they discovered the head of one of my uncles was too big for his neck. They asked him to think less— but that only made him dizzy.

To make sounds of footsteps in the snow, my father squeezed boxes of cornstarch.

A large contraption was suspended from the ceiling and placed around my uncle's head, trying to keep it balanced and contained. "Has anyone considered trepanation?" asked my brother.

My uncle was in danger of ceiling fans. When my father mentioned his airplane, my uncle ducked. A retired astronaut moved next door. He kept bumping into things. My uncle looked longingly at his astronaut's hat.

We discovered that sorrow was written in the margins of my grandmother's books. My sister collected excruciatingly small things. When the birds flew through winter, they tasted like snow.

The Thus Girl found her mouth at the end of my words.

Rain nailed the roof to the cellar. That was the year the candle company closed.

ASK THE BOOKS.
ASK THE DAMAGE.
ASK THE CANDLES.

The retired astronaut wore his lunar gloves and boots when he'd go out to get the mail—his backpack connected with umbilicals, his fish-bowl helmet cradled in his arms.

"I'll give you the sound of one hand clapping," said my father to my mother. People arrived behind their words. That was the year the world fell around us in different configurations. That was the year there was a crack in the ice. My father made bird sounds when he saw the bird sitting on the retired astronaut's Portable Life Support System backpack. My father made drilling sounds when he saw my uncle's large head.

The Thus Girl insisted it was a moth and I discovered holes nibbled in my sentences.

"What is your brother doing with that rock?" my mother asked.

My father made sounds as if he were walking away.

IN A HOUSE THAT WAS
MY BODY WAS A ROOM
THAT WAS MY LIFE.

The fire finally came. It came out of the toaster, out of the ceiling fan, out of the hair dryer, out of the spokes. The aquarium ignited into tiny tropical flames.

That was the year our father tried to be an Escape Artist. We'd tie him up. Shackle him. Handcuff him.

That was the year I walked around with a picture of a shaman.

The sky contained time. My brother had a dog named Nietzsche.

The birds flew off like pieces of chopped up scarves the day my grandmother was diagnosed with forgetfulness. Our neighbor was a puppeteer and everything was entangled in string. Dawn dragged itself through the town. That was the year I ate a hole in the window. The sky was abundant with birds and smoke.

The bees moved like flying jewels. We pushed death back

inside. The bees were agents exchanging nectar as they ate the space inside a flower.

The fountain burned.

We were the secret family—the one that had survived.

Everything smelled like the aftermath of fire.

The burnt smells came through the windows.

We moved the charred chairs beneath the charred table.

We remodeled the burning room—the rug of embers, the lamps glowed.

PICTURE (SHAMAN)

My grandmother found the recipe for her funeral cake, and my brother's dog died. I carried a staircase around with me as I moved around the ashes.

We heard a muffled sound struggling to get out of the fire.

THE DETECTIVE KNOCKED
ON THE DOOR AND ASKED
WHAT HAD HAPPENED.

That's when we decided to have a time capsule, and the mayor of the town was sad. We gathered items to include. We gathered the roads. We gathered the weather. We gathered the wanted posters in the post office, and the constellations behind the glass in the school.

After my grandfather died, my grandmother became a window.

And we gathered broken bits of glass.

That was the year I inhaled. That was the year I exhaled. My youngest sister was sick.

That was the year when a plane flew over the town the luggage door popped open, and suitcases and clothing fell through the sky. When people made comments about the weather, they talked about translucent scarves. Ties the color of blunt knives. The fields were covered in hats. Streets were covered in socks. Brassieres fell on the cemetery stones.

Our neighbors looked exactly like us. It was scary—they were a more complete version of us. Their house was the mirror image of our cellar.

I needed to talk to someone.

Our father was the negative image of our neighbor's father. Their house dreamed our cellar.

That was the year we studied consciousness in school though it was hard to stay awake. For the time capsule we gathered the mayor's sadness. We gathered my grandfather's cough and my grandmother's wobble.

As the clothing fell through the sky, the world seemed opened and buoyant. The weather was sublime and crazy, as a dress floated toward us—the color of sunburn.

For the time capsule, we gathered the weather.

We were the slumbering versions of our neighbor's waking. Their lives balanced on top of our lives.

For the time capsule, my father kept dying.
For the time capsule, my father wouldn't die.

"I WANT TO ONE DAY LIVE MY LIFE SO I CAN MAKE MY LOVER'S PSYCHIATRIST PROUD."

That was the year we discovered musical instruments scattered in the forest. I tried to put on the shoes of my dead grandfather, but they didn't fit. My foot kept slopping out of the big brown shoe.

That was the year we discovered a piano on top of a mountain. Things became attached. String. We pulled the day behind us.

After the stroke my grandmother became attached to silence. A star attached itself to the dark. A story attached itself to the world. My brother looked for a dirt road.

My uncle carried pictures of the seven deadly sins. "Why did you tell him that was a sin?" asked my mother.

That was the year my father was a prison guard, and he put bars on the cellar windows. In my uncle's pocket, an apparently naked woman peeked out from behind a parachute. "A warning," said my uncle. "More like a reminder," said my father.

Disease attached itself to healing. Food attached itself to some mouths. A stone attached itself to the cellar.

Wounds attached themselves to scars.

The hidden self attached itself to the revealed self.

The eye attached itself to objects.

I said, "I am starving." And my mouth attached itself to food.

Our neighbor was the sin-eater. Every time someone died, he would eat their sins. "Look how fat he is," said my uncle.

That was the year I crossed the line. All the objects we had purchased seemed to rot. The bird attached itself to the sky. The music attached itself to silence.

The sin-eater's mouth attached itself to the song my sister sang in the window.

And not long after, my grandfather's shoes became the dirt road.

OUR STORIES REPEAT THEMSELVES ENDLESSLY AROUND US—ULTIMATELY REVISING WHO WE ARE EVERY TIME.

At night when we approached the cellar we lived in, we could see the lights. It was as if a little house were being swallowed by the earth. It was as if there were a light on in the earth.

My father worked in the puzzle factory. There was an eerie glowing. That summer I got a job killing bees and had to spend the next summer praying for forgiveness.

My mother set out the stain glass eating utensils: the St. Francis carving knife, the St. Lidwinia fork, the St. Dymphna spoon.

We started gathering sandbags. We walked behind ventilation masks. We walked around with Geiger counters. My brother said he was going to be an existentialist and began to look curiously happy. We nailed plywood on the windows. We tested the water. We tested the soil. We tested the air. We tried not to breathe.

That was the year something was missing.

My brother said, "Dionysius is not a saint."

When our mother came home, she said she hit something with the car

"How could you?" Asked my father

"I don't know."

"What was it?"

"I don't know."

There was police tape around the neighbor's house. My brother said, "Daedalus is not a saint."

My father said, "You broke St. Dymphna. Now, we will never be able to eat." The termites carried the wooden parts of the town in their mouths. The metal parts began to rust. The glass parts started to crack.

I stared at the silence around my brother. "Now what can I do?" he asked. "I've become the wall I built to protect myself." He looked angrily at me. "Who will put the bees back?" he asked.

A mirror was being eaten.

A light was being devoured.

"Shatter me," I heard my sister say.

My father started crying at the kitchen table. Huge drops splattered in the bowl. "I can't stop," he said.

MAKING A LIST
OF ALL THE LISTS
THAT WERE MADE.

I made a list of phobias:

Chorophobia

Aulophobia

Optophobia

"All I do is make lists," I said to the However Girl. "You mean, like lists of things not to say to girls?" she asked. "Did you ever read the Kama Sutra?" asked my brother. "Yes, however, that should be on the list," said the However Girl.

Lists of tangled things.

Everything that is good.

Everything that is bad.

Things to say. Things not to say. Lists of gangster names.

Then I would get confused. "Legs Diamond." I would say to the girl. "What?" she'd ask. "Oh, I don't know. I was just thinking." "About legs?" "I don't know." "What are you, some kind of pervert?"

What do you call it when someone is afraid of a list?

    Phagophobia

    Pyrophobia

    Ecophobia

I made a list of astronaut's names, of Mayan gods, magicians, kinds of clouds, czars, wines, musical instruments. Wild Horses. Winding Dragons. Hovering Butterflies.

I carried my report card home:

Transfiguration	B
Epiphany	C+
Shamanism	D
Flute Playing	C-
Alchemy	I

Thanatophobic, my father made a list of all the ways he didn't want to die. My mother kept a list of women she would rather have been.

My brother kept a list of revolutionaries and visionaries. Bibliophobic, my youngest sister sat down and ate the lists.

Apiphobic, my grandmother opened her hand and a bee flew out.

THIS IS
THE DAWN
OF THE REST
OF OUR LIES.

That was the year my father was drunk. He stumbled into a train. He stumbled into a clock. He stumbled into a puzzle. Our home was broken into and someone stole all our clothes. Throughout the year, I saw people dressed as members of my family.

When my older sister woke, she was missing an eyebrow. My father was furious. "I had a dream where my boyfriend licked my eyebrow."

Our neighbors were the Choke family. The Tepid family. My brother told me the story of the UFO.

I saw my father's tie walk down the street. We danced like we were machinery. We watched our neighbors, and our neighbors watched us.

Our neighbors were the Transparent family. The Counterfeit family. The Cathartic family. The mayor was taller than his hair.

My father worked as a flagman for a road crew. He had the flags of all the countries. When he wanted the traffic to stop, he'd hold up Canada or Brazil or Bengladesh. Sometimes he'd wave a car on with Australia or Greece.

When my older sister woke, one of her eyes was a different color. "I had a dream where my boyfriend cried into one of my eyes."

That was the year the world wanted and wanted. That was the year the world decided to watch. My father stumbled into his brain.

My older sister dreamt she showed her boyfriend the bee in her mouth. He was fearful and amazed. I saw my mother's slip walk down the street. Our neighbors were the Hat family.

That was the moment I decided to fly.

My sister said her mouth tasted like smoke when it was over.

BIRDS NEVER
LEFT THE SKY.

That was the year when the world went away. That was the year we couldn't find the right words.

My father worked in a Wing Factory. "So what do you do exactly?" asked the priest.

I looked at the Because Girl. We were pulled into each other's gravitational force. My head felt like an empty pocket.

"What is there left to say?" asked my father. That was the year my father lost the keys. "Why do you keep putting sticks in your mouth?" asked my father.

I ate like a gnat.

The answer hid inside the question. My head felt like a birdhouse.

At the Air Show, we watched the wing walker. We were surprised how heavy the skydivers were. They clunked around the town.

That was the year we couldn't find the right worlds. My head felt like a beehouse. My head felt like a songhouse.

That was the year a terrible winged thing landed on the top of the church.

An animal lived in the forest and ate time.

The doctor said my father's organs had been terribly jumbled up as if he had fallen from a great height.

THE WORLD
OF MELTED
THINGS.

I read the *Book of Loss*. I learned to see inside people—to the opal, the pearl, the pit. Every dawn it was as if the town were made of glass and I'd been given a crystal hammer.

To help my sister study for a Psychology exam, she cut names of diagnoses and placed them on the kitchen table for members of the family to select. "If you insist on being happy," said my sister to my mother, "then you'll have to be bipolar."

"What's hebephrenia?" asked my brother.

It was noon.

My father was a cartographer, and rolled his maps out over the roof of the cellar. "This is where we are," he said, but his mouth was filled with uncertainty.

The skydiver hid inside the sky among the bottom dwelling clouds—among the cumulus body sacks. That was the year the tuba players came to town.

My neighbor was a bookie. My grandmother was a book.

My brother walked around with a name tag that said Depression.

When she heard what my family was doing, the Whatever Girl said she wanted to be a Borderline Personality Disorder.

With a name tag that said Narcissistic, my father stood in front of his crumbling maps. "Here," he said, and his finger trembled.

There was a noonful of sunlight.

I looked for the pieces of this created world.

I heard my parents talk about my brother's condition.

Every dawn it was as if the town were on fire, and I'd been given a match.

We ate pieces of dirt. The maps draped over the cellar roof, over the cellar windows—rectangles of dust.

Our house was covered with all the places of the world. Our cellar contained all the strangenesses of the world.

My father handed my neighbor some money.

In school we studied why the universe had organized itself into so many diverse things. Something joyful sat above us.

THE TOWN
DETERMINES
WHAT THIS MEANS.

Q. What did the father do for a living?
A.

Q. What happened once we lost our ability to communicate with animals?
A. We lost our souls.

Q. What are you eating?
A.

Q. What did the brother say after his UFO abduction?
A. It was like being in a sky lit chapel, except for the probes.

Q. What do you do when you live in a cellar?
A. You pray to the dirt-god.

Q. Who wears a parachute while riding an escalator?
A. My father wore a parachute while climbing a ladder.

Q. Then what happened?

A. Each book in my grandmother's bookcase followed language into death—word by word.

Q. How long will nature tolerate us?

A.

Q. Is it true that one of the uncle's penises was stung by a bee?

A. A note was slipped under the door of my dream.

Q. Do you have a melancholic desire for the absent other?

A. Yes.

Q. Were the neighbors from Bulgaria, Nigeria, or Thailand?

A. Yes.

Q. Did the mayor destroy the map?

A.

Q. Was the cellar the root of the house?

A. It was an inverted blossom.

Q. Did you eat like a bee?

A. I ate like a sparrow.

Q. Did you read the *Book of Shattering*?

A. I read the *Book of Holes*.

Q. What happened to the brother? What happened to the mother? What happened to the two sisters? Is it true about the father? What does it mean?

A.

MY MOTHER LOOKED UP
THE EXPIRATION DATE
FOR THE HOLY WATER.

Because my mother believed there would be a miracle, she bought lottery tickets at the gas station and placed plastic saints in the backyard. A picture of Mary was clipped to the clothesline so it would rain. And my mother said it was a miracle. The picture of Mary started to cry just at the moment it began to rain.

My mother referred to the Crying Goddess. My aunt's ring was like a sore, and she thought my mother referred to her. Tears fell on the tarpaper roof of the cellar and the house began to grow.

In school we studied how the world would end. We made a list and then had to choose. I preferred the meteor over the super volcano.

Our neighbors were foreign and said something about a white deer. My father was a ventriloquist. "I am not moving my lips," he said as he moved his lips.

That was the year we tried to rescue the story out of the words. Our next door neighbors kept a starving child in the front yard. After all was said and undone, we were the secret family. The starving child's eyes were bigger than its belly.

Our neighbors said, "This is our word for sky. This is our word for word."

Words hid in my grandmother's books. That was the year when everything started over again—when home could not find its way back. That was the year the wounds turned to rust, and the one rose that grew next to the cellar looked more like a scab.

The letters arrived in the mail, and the TV said: More of this.
"Stop it," said my mother to the mayor. "Just stop it."
The dummy that looked like my brother slumped in a chair.

I preferred nuclear winter to global warming. When I entered my grandmother's house, words hid in her books. Our neighbors were indigenous. And my uncle said we should be afraid of them. "Sky Gardeners," my father called them.

In our neighbor's front yard, rain fell into the starving child's eyes. That was the year the white deer appeared at the edge of the woods.

WE CALLED
THE CELLAR
THE WELL-WOUND.

A shaman moved next door. In school we studied the souls
of objects. Some floated behind the object like a shadow. Some
were muffled as if they had been swallowed. Some sizzled like
electricity in the throat.

My mother said, "Don't be afraid."

It was harder than I thought to distinguish what was easy to
swallow and what was hard to swallow.

Staying up all night with my grandmother's sewing kit, my
mother made wings for my sister. "This is for your own good,"
said my father.

Our neighbor was shaped like a cement mixer.

Where the cellar lived there was more gravity. I slumped
under my school books.

I worried about multiplication. How many of me would
there be by the end of the day if I wasn't careful.

When I heard my father come home, I'd barricade the door. A thorn tree twisted through the backyard. We stumbled into time. The one neon sign blistered in the town.

My grandmother became more adept at forgetting. When I went out to the beehouse to see what had been left behind, my mother said, "Don't be afraid."

I waved to the shaman from behind our fence. "Be a gate," the Shaman said.

Night moved into the town like a deer.

ASK THE DIRT.
ASK THE FALLEN HOUSE.
ASK THE SKY.

That was the year my father swam, and he showed me how to tilt my head and shake the opposite leg in order to get water out. That was the year I discovered a hidden river.

"I am hiding in these words."

The Shaman exchanged information between the upper and lower world. He watched my sister fly off to the school play.

I slept with a pen in bed with me, and when I woke up this is what was written on my body.

**THIS IS
A TUMBLE
STORY.**

I carried maps of places we destroyed. In spite of this, all around me there were little bursts of beauty, and I discovered a parachute in my parent's closet.

I COULD HEAR THE HEART BEATING IN THE CLOUDS.

"Why are we doing fire drills? We live in a cellar," I said.

"Who do you think you are?" said my father.

"We are trying to escape the fire of the house that once burned above us," said my mother.

"Just because there is no smoke doesn't mean there is no fire," said my older sister.

I COULD HEAR THE HEART BEATING IN THE DIRT.

That was the year I discovered the world in my grandmother's books. That was the year I ate nothing. The houses of the town collapsed inside themselves.

My father was a marshaller on the ramp of our town's airport. He'd guide the planes next to the gates.

Our neighbor was an acupuncturist, and there were pins all over the yard.

I COULD HEAR THE HEART BEATING IN THE WOODS.

My brother said a house is easier to build than a novel, but a novel is easier to live in. Words were made of worlds.

My father stood in the dark—orange flashlight wands grew out of his hands.

I COULD HEAR THE HEART BEATING IN THE WORDS.

In school we determined what was alive.

That was the year I discovered the world was made of words.

I wrote a story where I finally died.

That was the year I started eating books.

I heard a voice, "If I don't come down, send up a rescue team to find me."

THAT WAS
THE YEAR
MY FATHER
FELL OUT OF
THE SKY.

My father was drunk and sleeping. We tried not to speak because if we woke him he would roar. No one could figure out who had chopped down the fruit tree. That was the year I read the *Book of Ends*.

Something terrible was about to happen. My grandmother's bookcase melted.

The boy hid inside the cellar.

The cellar hid inside the house.

The house hid inside the town.

The town hid inside the boy.

That was the year my mother was elected mayor.

I watched the way the birds plucked the air.

I asked my grandmother if she had a book that contained nature. She opened her hand and showed me the rivers and ditches, the death lines and dirt roads.

That was the year I just couldn't stop. Tomorrow drank up today. Yesterday drank up tomorrow. That was the year I just couldn't stop.

I learned that words when repeated led to a resonance creating a vibrational adjustment on the molecular level—thus establishing a detectable radiance. I repeated: When I stand inside my sacred power, I am strong.

I wanted to write a book where the whole book was the dream of a dead man. "It's been done," said my father. "Just ask your dead grandfather."

"OK," I said. "But my book would be so poorly written no one would ever know it was a dead man dreaming."

"Perfect," said my father. And I thought that would be the end of it.

"I am afraid I will find a book with my picture in it," I said to my grandmother, and death untied the knot that held my grandfather to the town.

Tomorrow moved brokenly ahead of us. It wore a peculiar hat. It said: I am here to tell you…. It wore a parachute.

My sister stood in the place where the tree had been chopped down.

I WAS WRITING
A BOOK CALLED
THE BOOK OF WONDER.

I was writing a book called *The Last Book*.
My brother left a note on the kitchen table. It said:
> REALIZATION
> INTEGRATION
> ACTIVATION
> LIBERATION

The sky had eaten the house. Our dead grandmother came to live with us. I turned into Ovid. In music class in school I studied the flute. They called me to pick up my father from the insane asylum. "He's acting crazy," they said.

When my mother went to sleep, birds flew out of her head.

Our neighbors had sex during *I Love Lucy*.

That was the year my brother attempted suicide. I turned into *The Last Book*. I turned into the fire that was eating the town.

Songs of the birds tore up the sky.

That was the year we studied phobias. That was the year we studied limerence. It goes without saying that we were afraid to watch my mother sleeping.

There were burn marks on the towels. My father prayed to the dirt gods. My uncle prayed to the fire gods.

After I ate a caterpillar, it emerged as a butterfly. Did the words belong to the books, or did the books belong to the words?

Our neighbors had sex during *The World News*.

"Will you be the person I write for?" I asked the Nevertheless Girl. I asked if she would feed me poetry. The word "love" grew inside my mouth.

"What if it's too late?" my brother said. We studied the unraveling.

Did I belong to the town or did the town belong to me? Our neighbors had sex during J. D. Salinger.

In school we studied the dead gods.

I turned into a scarecrow.

I turned into a bird. I turned into a boy with a flute.

FROM THE SKY:
AN ECHO.

ASK THE BONES	ASK THE BONES
ASK THE MOUTH	ASK THE MOUTH
ASK THE ANIMALS	ASK THE ANIMALS

Birds walked all over the sky. The TV said: Reporting from Afghanistan. Reporting from Ghana.

The story hid inside the story. My grandfather hid inside his dying. The fetus hid inside her birth. That was the year the teacher decided to tell us the truth. The TV said: Reporting from Chile.

That was the year we watched our grandmother die. That was the year we watched our grandmother thrive.

I flew into the When Girl and she flew into me. A juice flowed through the town. The TV said: Reporting from Thailand.

My teacher said: "Our stories must be transformative." My teacher said: "I call on the birds." My teacher said: "Fathomlessly yours." The rain hid inside the river. The river hid inside the earth.

In school we studied the communal brain of the town.

The cellar snored beneath the earth. There was a cellar beneath the cellar—a stone stairway that went deeper. My mother said, "Soon the house will blossom from the blueprints." The mayor named the road in front of our house Saint St. The TV said: Reporting from India. Reporting from Malaysia.

My grandmother said there is a god who loves us and there is a god who hates us.

My father rolled out a map of an invisible country.

I read the *Book with the Hole in It*. The TV said: Reporting from the world.

The town began to speak with one mouth. I asked if I could have a new name. "Of course, Kokopelli," said my father.

We found a jump suit in the backyard. It appeared wings had been sewn on the shoulders.

ASK THE WORLD

ASK THE EARTH

THE TRICKSTER
PREPARES THE MAPS
OF THE IMAGINED WORLD.

The town balanced on the tips of the words in my grandmother's books.

In the Dream Palace, the same movie kept playing with nobody viewing it. Eventually it evolved into something else. The actors began to forget their lines.

That was the year the snow kept falling—sensuous, blissful, and disturbing. That was the year I read the *Book of Emptiness*.

A ribbon was buoyant in my sister's hair.

My father worked with mirrors.

The TV said: A child is missing in the woods.

My sisters were digging a hole through the snow. They took things out of it. They put things inside it.

My grandmother had a recipe for bees. She never knew my father built birdcages and terrariums.

The part of my youngest sister's life she hadn't lived unspooled before her. She went to the Dream Palace and memorized the actors' lines.

The town balanced between resurrection and complete wreckage while my father placed his mirrors everywhere.

The town was time-stained. It is hard to grasp the amount of darkness—especially at noon. In school we studied explorers. The sun was a beautiful scab.

A house was built around the family.

My sisters dug a white hole. The TV said: A child is missing in the words. One of the actors said, "Is it possible to love anymore?"

ASK THE TONGUE
ASK THE FLESH

If I sat on the map I would become a place, and eventually they would pull the town out of me.

After my grandfather died my grandmother ate from a broken plate.

The town balanced on the tip of a flame. Birds invented the sky. The pocket invented the clock. My grandmother ate my grandfather's picture.

Vasco de Gamma. Cortez. Balboa. The explorers never arrived. A ribbon drowned in my sister's hair.

A child fell into the hole in the backyard.

One of my grandmother's books was being eaten by another book.

The actors on the screen in the Dream Palace began to improvise.

The town balanced on a bee sting.

My father said he learned to walk inside the water like a fish.

I spent my time listening for the sweet crash of sticks.

Snow cried into the blank pages of a book. Carrying his mirrors, my father said, "That's the trick."

My grandmother began the unspooling.

Someone knocked at the door. When I opened it, there was a stranger. He said his name was Magellan.

A hole appeared where the house should have been.

The town balanced on the tip of my grandmother's memory.

Someone knocked at the door. When I opened it, there was a stranger. He said he was my father.

The man who said he was my father said he was an entomologist who spent his time dissecting bees.

I WAS WRITING
A BOOK CALLED
RESCUERS OF SKYDIVERS
SEARCH AMONG THE CLOUDS.

My younger sister learned how to talk to the neighbor's horse. My oldest sister told us she was pregnant, and my mother looked for the fetus in my dead grandmother's books.

For days we searched the sky, and nothing fell.

Once we saw how big the hole was we tried frantically to fill it up.

The mayor named the streets after body parts—Pineal Way.

My father lived on a boat on a river that changed colors— the murky color of the dirt, the diamond color of the sky.

The saddest part of the story is the town burned down. Shops made of smoke, churches made of smoke, bars and libraries and hardware stores made of smoke. My mother stood in the backyard and pointed her finger in the air, providing the birds with directions around the clouds.

ASK THE HOUSE.

ASK THE FAKE HOUSE.

ASK THE BURNING HOUSE.

The town became the body of my father and smoke rose above us.

There were more keys than doors.

I'm not sure at what point we realized we were the actors in the movie on the screen in the Dream Palace Theater, but once we did, among the beautiful and ruined, we gave the performance of our lives.

My father became the river that was under the boat. My father fished in the middle of a book.

My brother left a letter on the kitchen table. Nothing. To write home. About.

My grandmother's books shattering into words, the family began to eat the stones of the cellar. When we lived next to the burning factory, the family began to eat smoke. My brother said, "The journey begins with the end of the road." He stood with his mouth open, and another road seemed to blossom from it. I read the *Book of Bees* in a smoke filled cellar.

Music came out of the stick I had in my mouth.

My father's boat was the cellar.

The fetus grew in my grandmother's books. The parachute was a silk cloud. A floating rooftop. A fallen house.

The cellar became the body.
Became my mother.

I STRAP ON
THESE WORDS

And jump.

ACKNOWLEDGMENTS

For being part of the Search:
George Kalamaras Kirsten Kaschock Michael Burkard Paul B. Roth
Linda Pennisi David Lloyd Jeffrey Ethan Lee Martha Rhodes Nadxi
Nieto Hall Kathryn Rantala Paul Griner Chris Kennedy Barbara
Moore Clarkson Genevieve Nordmark Diane Wald Betsy Hogan
Benette Whitmore Ann Fisher-Wirth Susan Terris Mary Stebbins
Taitt Phil LaMarche Brent Goodman Tom Friedman Judith Johnson
Malena Mörling Kim Waale Tara Taylor Heather Hemmes Michelle
Gluck Jenny Ryan Matt Adams Jim Williamson John Ruskowski Terry
Reilly Sean Thomas Dougherty Laura Eiselen Thad Rutkowski John
Bradley Mary Slechta Phil Memmer Deborah Poe Ashley Farmer Ryan
Ridge Arielle Greenberg Joe Milford Chenelle Milford Sherry Fairchok
Jennifer MacPherson Bin Ramke Jake Adam York Natalie Anderson
Paul Aviles Rachel Guido DeVries Raina Von Waldenburg Mary-Ellen
Kavanagh Janine DeBaise Jennifer LaGraffe Mary Ann Samyn Ryan
Gangemi Mary Ann Cain Michael Sickler Georgia Popoff Lauren
Gibbs Eric Fisher Jessica Ortiz José Rico Richard Peabody Carra
Stratton Julie Olin-Ammentorp Tony Eallonardo Susan Clarke Cathy
Anderson Naomi Horii Patty Paine Christine Fennessy Sarah Kulpa
Carolyn Ramsden Katie Rose Goloski Jaime Hazard Brian Brodeur
Joe Smith Matt Attanasia Sandra Kelley Alex Gherardi Steve Huff
Cara Keenan Jeff Van Driessen Jordan Judd Griffin Hamell Mark
Garland Roger Hecht Steve Mullane Jess Maggi Staci Dennis Tanith
Callicoatt Fiona Barbour Allison Ehrhart Tamara Keeney Annie
Lighthart Ginger Knowlton Celie Katovitch Dolly Katovitch Philip
Booth WD Snodgrass Jim Vanderpool Ashlee Anno Elinor Cramer
Gerry LaFemina Chuck Hickey Tim Runk James Fitzgibbons Michael
Jennings Dan Roche Anna Blake Gary Lawless Susan Robinson
Emanuel Carter Khristopher Dodson Colleen Ghee Sara Mattise
Sarah Heukrath Robin Kimmerer William Noon Courtney Queeney
Sharon Moran Johnny Robinson Don Wagner Shreyas Roy Tom
McGrath Maureen Fitzsimmons Karel Blakeley Evan Thomas Betsy
Elkins Bob Lietz Beth Twiddy Phil Memmer Donna Steiner Valerie
Luzadis Rick Smardon Brendan Gilligan John Felleman Sue Senecah
Ann Ryan Julie Grossman Steve Alexander Tom Fogarty Sylvia
O'Connor Jill Evans Patti Gibeault Patty Kielecki Chris Crysler Suzy
Beardsley Leo Qaqish Rhiannon Williams Terry LeCasse Yvonne
Caine Candace Conrad Anjalee Nadkarni Jim MacKillop Olesya Vernyi
Bethany Rocine John Bellinger Dylan Blakeley Bill Morris Danny Fire
Trinity Mathis Alice Chanthasensak Lennie Decerce Basil Dillon-
Malone Denise Gasiorowski Shannon Firth Adam Desnoyers Joan

Cofrancesco Kathleen Poliquin Peter Lockwood Christine Ennis Lucy Harrison Barbara Grosso David Guilfoyle Brenda Nordenstam Amy Dieffenbacher Allie Randall James Butler David Sonnenfeld Dawnelle Jager Marianne Patinelli-Dubay Brenton Finizio Carol Courtwright Nate O'Neil Matthew Deavir Charlie Hall Cathy Gibbons Rand Bishop Mary Ann Keenan Anne-Marie Cusac Myrna Hall Jack Manno Carolyn Ryder Mark Meisner Bonnie Charity Mary Demetrick Cosima Bisslessi Kristin Ryan Orlando Ocampo Chris Warner Kathy Mack Linda Loomis Lennie DiFino Melissa Scobell Josh Thomas James Murphy Ashley O'Mara Sean Pratt Miles Slechta Peter Keith-Slack John Janitz Sarah Janus Chris Burgess David Dodd Lee Keri Wertz Teresa Gilman Terri Resch-Vickery Mary Bush Pat Sgroi Lisa LaFranco Karen Moore Roma Estevez Marianne Hirschfeld David Ripper Wendy Bishop Ann Carter Camlyn Valdez Suntrana Allen Jake Ellison Joe Bates Gia Capriotti Alex Di Rienzo David Feldman Nicole Moss Tina Limpert Renato Rosaldo Jill Greene Gordon Boudreau Madison Ava

For providing Clouds:
Paul B. Roth and *The Bitter Oleander* where two sections of the novel were published.

For being among the Rescuers:
Carra Stratton, Kirsten Kaschock, Genevieve Nordmark, Ashley Farmer, and Linda Pennisi for having read, responded to, commented on, and offered suggestions and early support.

For helping the Skydivers:
Kate Bernheimer and Dan Waterman who brought the book to life.